Big and Little

by Jane Ouellette

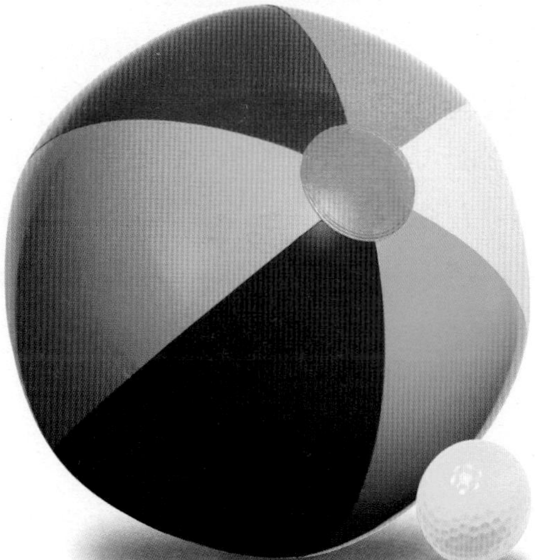

HOUGHTON MIFFLIN BOSTON

To the Teacher

This wordless book focuses on developing vocabulary for size words such as *big* and *little*.

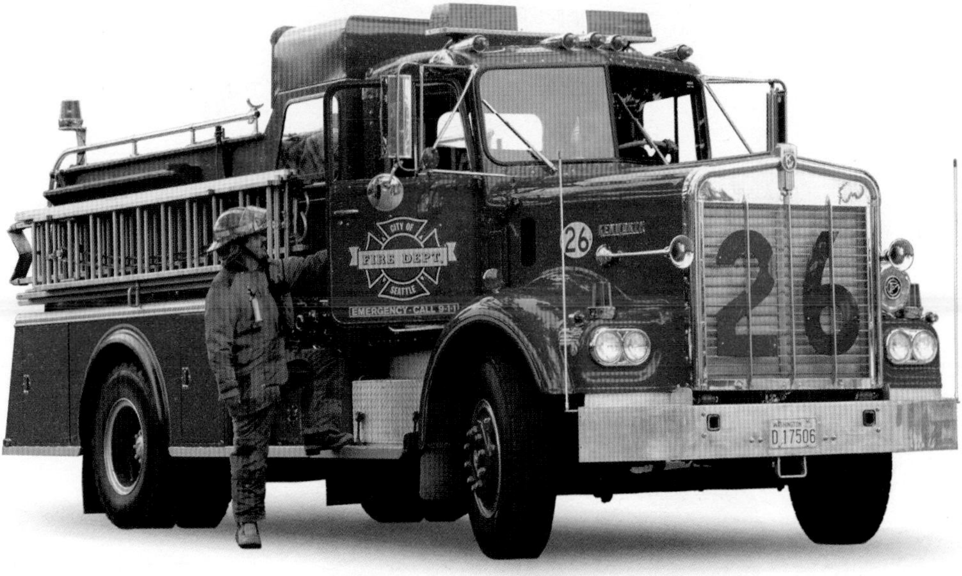
CITY OF
FIRE DEPT.
SEATTLE
EMERGENCY-CALL 9-1-1
26
26
D 17506

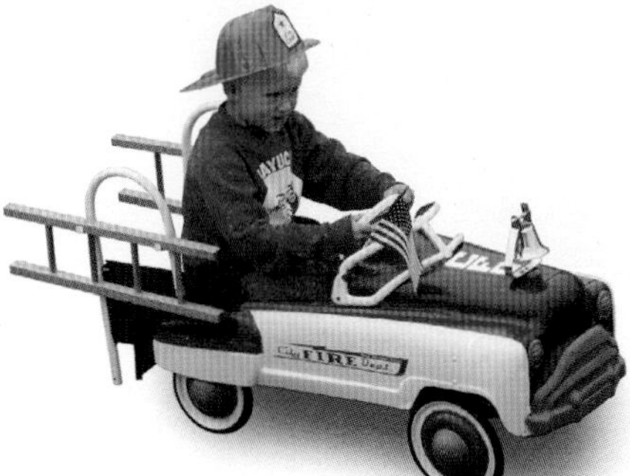
FIRE

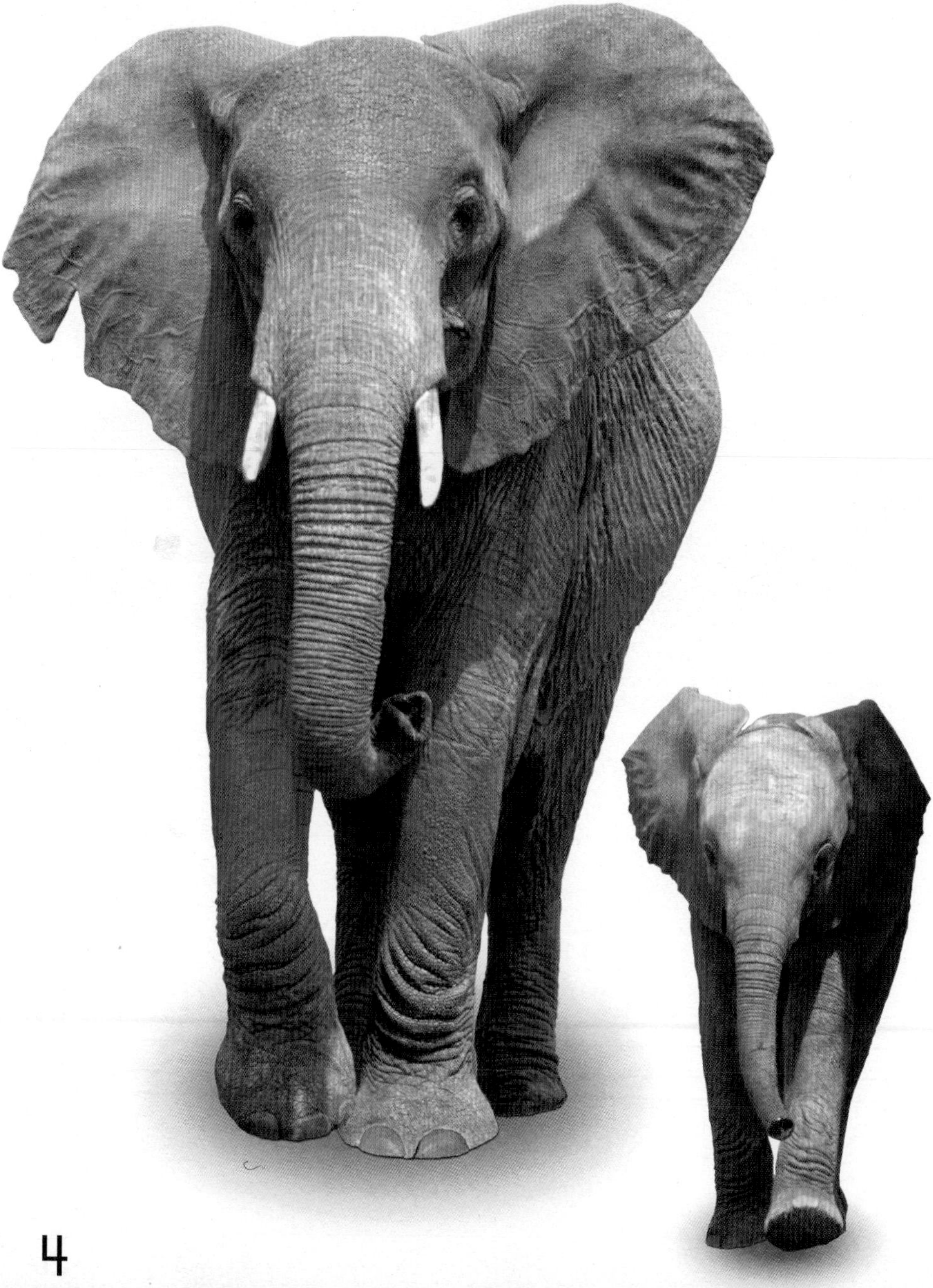

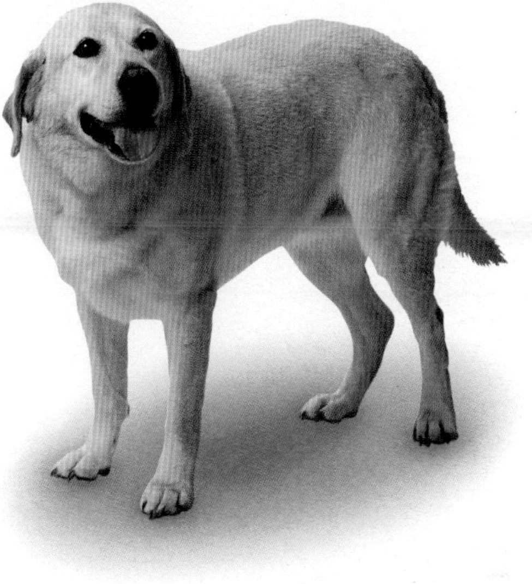

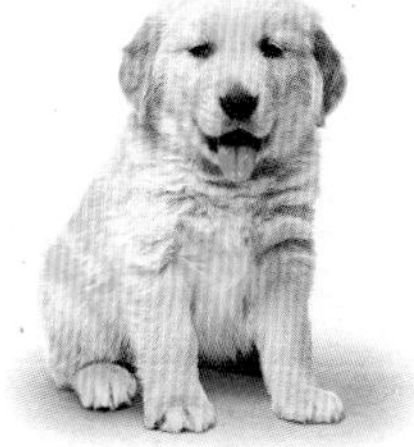

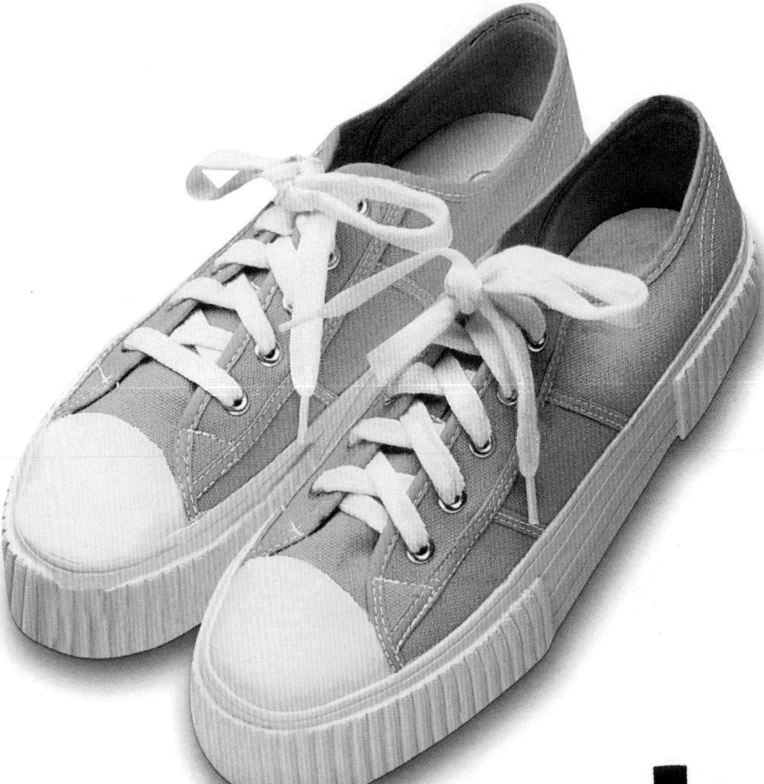

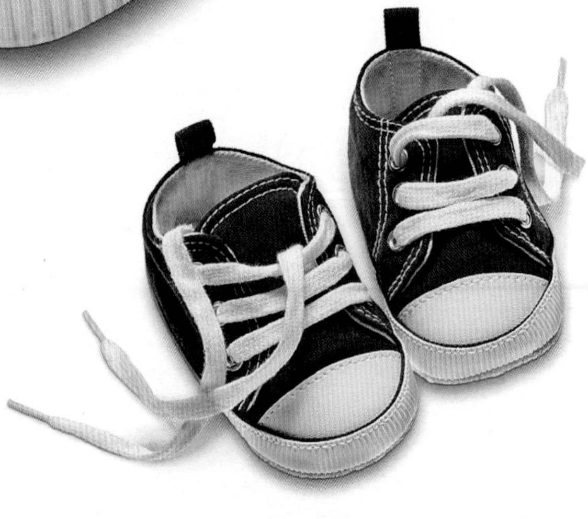

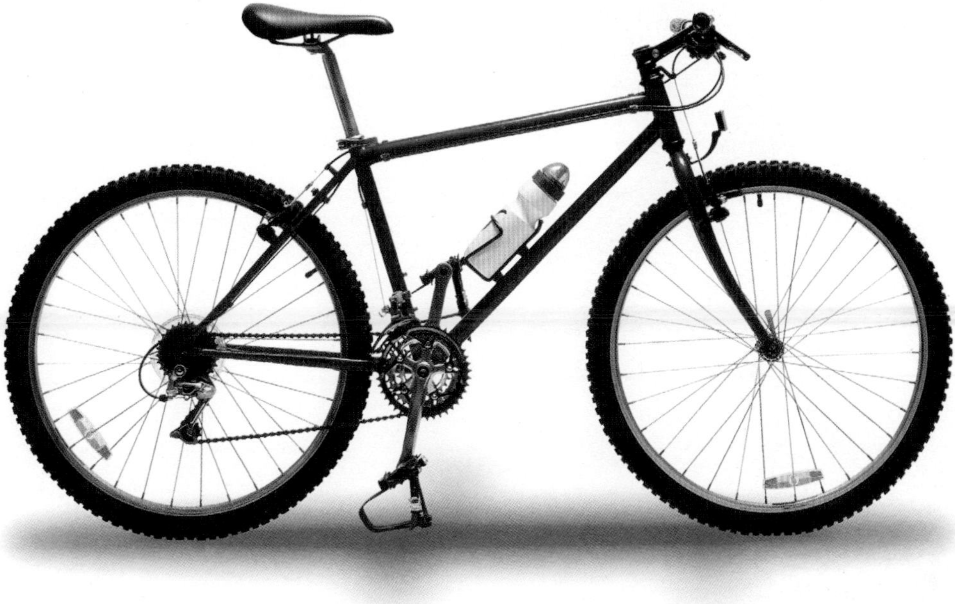

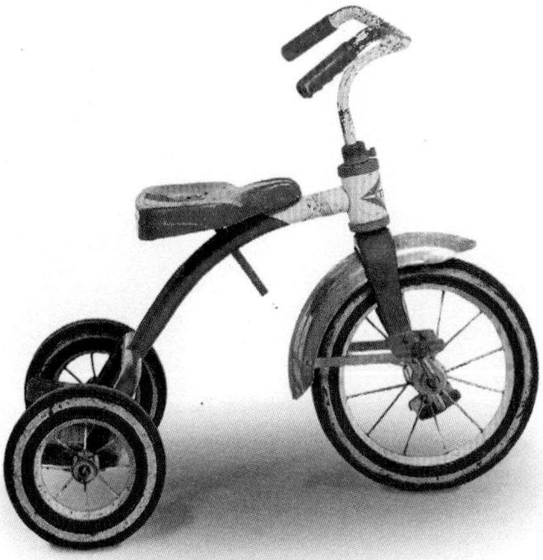

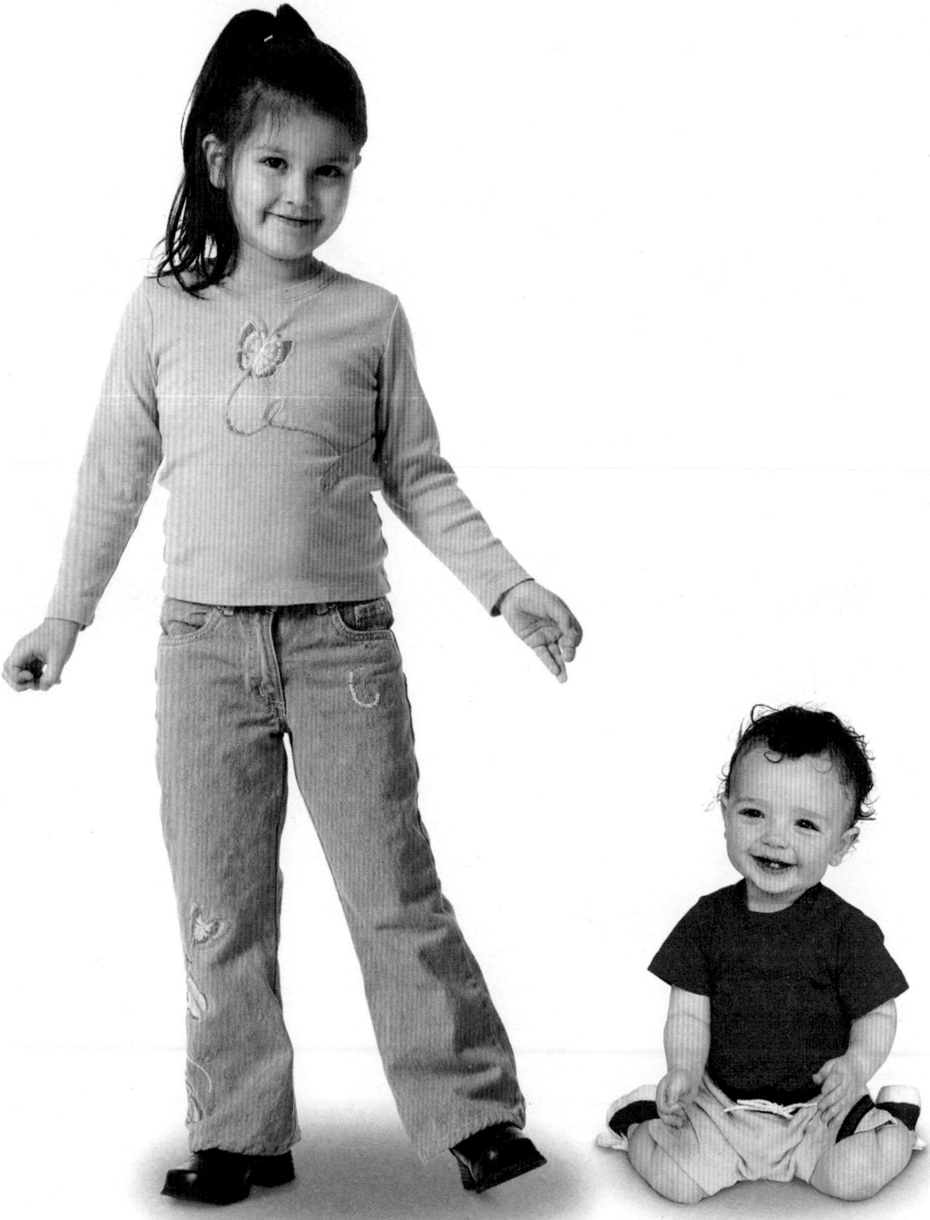